JUL 0 8 2015

PETLANDIA

PETER HANNAN

Scholastic Press · New York

For Gizmo, Stella, Scat, Honeybaked Hamster, Scarface, Billy Joe Bob Jr., Billy Joe Bob Jr. Jr., Peeper, Peeve, Steve, Scram, Ping, Pong, Blackie, Binker, Binker II, and Tipper the 3-Legged Dog

Copyright © 2015 by Pete Hannan

Library of Congress Cataloging-in-Publication Data

Hannan, Peter, author.
 Petlandia / by Peter Hannan.
  pages cm

Summary: Feline Madame Wigglesworth is outraged when her privileged position in the house is usurped by a mere dog, Grub, so she comes up with a plan to expel the humans and put the pets, namely herself, in charge—but their human-free realm soon dissolves into complete chaos as she and Grub and his lovestruck sidekick Honeybaked Hamster struggle for the presidency.

ISBN 978-0-545-16211-1

1. Cats—Juvenile fiction. 2. Dogs—Juvenile fiction. 3. Hamsters—Juvenile fiction. 4. Animals—Juvenile fiction. 5. Humorous stories. [1. Cats—Fiction. 2. Dogs—Fiction. 3. Hamsters—Fiction. 4. Pets—Fiction. 5. Humorous stories.] I. Title.

PZ7.H1978Pe 2015
813.54—dc23
[Fic]

2014048230

10 9 8 7 6 5 4 3 2 1   15 16 17 18 19

Printed in the U.S.A.   23

First edition, May 2015

Book design by Christopher Stengel

CHAPTER ONE

Madame Wigglesworth didn't always hate the humans.

She actually almost tolerated the Finkleblurts when they treated her properly: like the queen she knew she was.

They worshipped her from afar.

Just the way a queen likes it.

But one day the unthinkable occurred. She got dethroned.

The dethroner was a lovable, dim, and totally insane little pup named Grub.

The very first thing Grub did was eat Madame Wigglesworth's crown. But did he get punished? Hardly.

He grew up fast. Every single day, the humans showered him with love, something Madame Wigglesworth found painful to watch. Grub slobbered, they cooed. He messed, they cheered. He did the most basic stuff, like sitting, rolling over, or fetching a spit-soaked ball, and they danced around the room like wacky windup toys.

It's like they're awarding gold medals for breathing, she thought.

Then there was the endless belly rubbing. The humans seemed to worship that belly, like it had some kind of magical power. Madame Wigglesworth was horrified.

This is deeply embarrassing for everyone involved, she thought. *Love and affection are for suckers. Highly developed individuals such as myself do not want or need them.*

Some might think I'm jealous, but how could one possibly be jealous of such a pitiful creature?

But of course she was jealous. She had never craved belly rubbing in her life, but now she was obsessed with it. Sometimes you don't want something until you see somebody else getting it.

And Grub was getting it **big-time**.

Halloween was the final straw. The humans dressed the animals in costumes—something pet owners should never, ever, ever do. But at least they put together a super look for Grub.

Madame Wigglesworth's getup was of the decidedly unsuper variety.

This is no accident. They're out to get me. I mean, do I seem like the type to wear a rainbow wig, a rubber nose, and size twenty-seven shoes? Not to mention the hottest, pinkest, ugliest pants this side of Hot-Pink-Pants Uglytown?

Madame Wigglesworth couldn't take it anymore.

She suffered a little breakdown.

Diagnosis: "stark-raving nutjob-itis."

Second opinion: "Aggravated Wackadoodle Disorder."

Her symptoms were clear: chattering teeth, itchy eyeballs, whisker wilt, fur fungus, tingly tail, critter cramp, tabby trauma, and kitty quakes. Not to mention irritated claw syndrome and an ingrown hair ball.

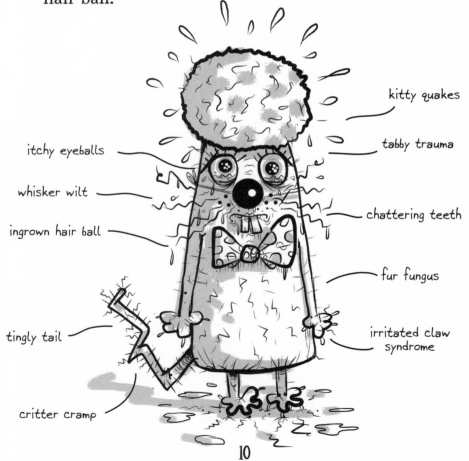

kitty quakes

tabby trauma

itchy eyeballs

whisker wilt

ingrown hair ball

chattering teeth

fur fungus

tingly tail

irritated claw syndrome

critter cramp

She was delirious with hurt and hate. She threw herself face-first onto the couch and meowed into the cushion for forty-five minutes. Then came lots of blubbering and sniveling. She cried approximately thirty gallons of tears.

CHAPTER TWO

But then a very nasty lightbulb clicked on in Madame Wigglesworth's head. She had an idea—a very sneaky idea.

"What do I want? Revenge! When do I want it? Now!!!"

Sometimes it takes a while for a scheme to formulate, but not this time. A perfectly diabolical three-step plan had popped into her head, fully formed and beautifully, simply evil.

"Step one is Grub," she whispered. "I hate the mutt with every fiber of my being, but I hate the humans ten times more. They are the real disease. Grub is merely a symptom, and symptoms are easily treated . . . like a bad rash.

"Yoo-hoo! Grub! You bad rash, you! I mean, good friend! Can I have a word?"

"Sure," said Grub. "Which word does you want?"

"No, no," said Madame Wigglesworth. "I mean, can we talk?"

"I kinda busy right now. I is dreaming of a meatball from the trash that's bluish and whitish and fuzzy-ish that I saw two minutes or five years ago." Grub had a terrible sense of time.

"Yeah," said Honeybaked Hamster, entering the room and eyeballing the cat suspiciously. "Grub dreams a lot. That's 'cause he is **dreamy. Dream-o-licious.** A total **dreamsicle.** A one-dog **dream team.**" Honeybaked had a small crush on Grub. "He's too busy to chitchat with the likes a you."

Madame Wigglesworth closed her eyes and counted to ten, twice. Controlling her temper was an important part of the plan. "Listen, Grub. You know when the humans laugh when you're around? Well, they're not laughing *with* you."

Grub cracked up. "Okay, well that unpossible! If I is *around*, then I is *with* them. So the laughing isn't someplace else. It with me! Madame W, is you feeling okay? Because you seems a tiny bit wackadoodle or even slightly nutjobby."

"I heard them talking!" She moved in closer. "They said, 'From now on, there will be absolutely no more belly rubs for Grub!'"

This got Grub's attention. "You mean they means no more, like no more than, say, four or five belly rubs a day?"

"No, Grub, I mean they mean no more like *no more. Ever.* No rubbing, no patting, no contact of any kind, belly-wise! They *despise* the belly! They detest the belly! They joined Belly Haters Not-at-all Anonymous!"

"But why?!" moaned Grub. "Was it that turkey or the fancy-schmancy couch?!"

Last Thanksgiving, Grub had eaten the entire bird and half of the brand-new sofa.

"No," said Wigglesworth, "it's just you. Y-O-U. They simply do not like *you* anymore."

"But . . . but . . . even if they don't likes somebody they still could prolly rub somebody's belly, right?"

Madame Wigglesworth lost it. "NO! Say good-bye to the belly-rubbing era! It's over! Finished! Kaput! You get it?"

Grub finally got it.
He also got woozy.

Very woozy.

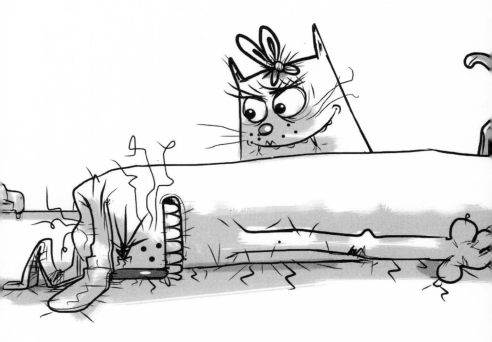

He collapsed in a heap.

"Somebody call an ambulance!" shrieked Honeybaked.

"Hold on, Hammy," said Madame Wigglesworth. "We animals should stick with our own kind. We'll take care of Grub. Besides, he's fine. He's just a little sensitive about the humans hating him out of the blue for no reason. Well, not for no reason. I mean, *look* at him."

"I *am* looking at him," said Honeybaked. "Isn't he gorgeous with his nose all crinkled up and that teeny bit of drool on his lip?"

"Yes, yes," said Wigglesworth, gagging slightly. "He's an angel." She stroked Grub's head and talked softly into his ear. "Now, now, pup-pup, don't you worry your pretty little echo chamber of a head about this. Auntie Wigglesworth has an idea."

Grub opened one eye. "You has an idea?" he asked with a whimper. "Good, because I checked my brainy and it's full of something that doesn't seems like an idea."

Madame Wigglesworth smiled. The very same cluelessness that once disgusted her now delighted her.

"Not to worry," she whispered. "I have enough ideas for the both of us. And not just ideas, a *plan!*"

"Sounds good," said Clowny, the depressed clown fish, watching from his aquarium. "And by 'good' I mean very, very bad." He was always a little worried that Madame Wigglesworth might eat him, and he didn't even consider that the worst thing about her.

CHAPTER THREE

Mr. Finkleblurt snored loudly, as usual. How Madame Wigglesworth despised him. But it would all be over soon.

Time for step two.

BONG! BONG! The clock bonged twelve times, but Madame Wigglesworth got impatient after two.

"It's midnight, people! It was midnight at bong one! It's time for my perfectly plotted rebellion against the humans! No more lollygagging! Riot! Revolt! Let the revolution begin!"

"I wish I could!" bubbled Clowny, his face smushed up against the glass. "I don't get to go anywhere, unless you call a one-inch swim followed by a painful smack in the face going somewhere."

"GRUB!" screamed Madame Wigglesworth.

"IT'S GO TIME!"

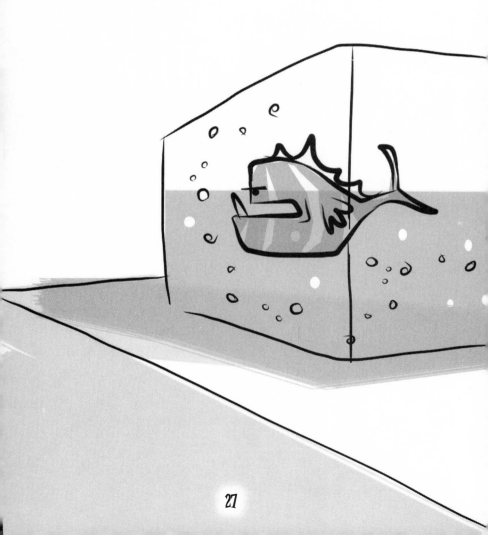

"ROGER, WIGGLESWORTH! I'M GO-TIMING!" cried Grub, leaping into action, crawling across the living room floor like a furry commando.

Honeybaked Hamster was so excited, her goose bumps had goose bumps. "Now I have a inklings of what General George Washington's men musta feeled when theys crossin' the Smellaware! 'Cept they prolly didn't get to ride on his back! Onward, General Grub!"

"That's right, Private Honeybaked," said Grub. "Not 'zactly sure what revolution is, but it gotta be a lot more pleasanter than not getting your belly rubbed forever and ever!"

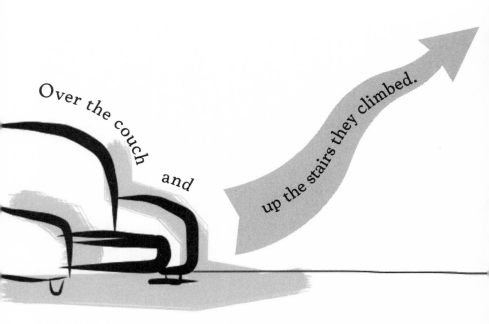

Over the couch and up the stairs they climbed.

They tiptoed to the Finkleblurts' bedrooms. Grub got mad when he saw the humans up close.

"Go ahead and sleep likes you thinks I gots no idea about your new outrage-erous no-belly policy!

"You gonna wake up and smell the music soon, 'cause the times they are a-changin'!"

He quietly dragged the mattresses, one by one, with his teeth, down the hallway to the top of the stairs.

"I was so wrong about you, General Grub," said Honeybaked. "You not a super genius at all. You a super-dee-*duper* genius."

Someday I'll gets up the courage to tell him I loves him, and worships him, and models my whole life after him, she thought.

But that day was not today.

"One, two, three . . . push!" ordered Madame Wigglesworth. *Oh, what joy,* she thought, *having a couple of fabulous flunkies doing one's dirty work!*

With a mighty heave, the mattresses were airborne.

"Wheeeeee!" squealed hound and hamster, riding the last two like floppy surfboards.

"Gnarly pipeliney of bodacious-ness!" howled Grub. He had watched a few surfing movies and knew the lingo. Sort of. "I'm in my pockets!"

"How does you get in your pockets?" asked Honeybaked. "We don't even has *pants!*"

"Gee . . . looks like fun," moaned Clowny.
"Something I have never had. Ever."

"Revolution!" screamed Madame Wigglesworth.

"I'm a rebelooshinary!" cheered Grub.

"You're revolting!"

"Yes, I'm revolting!"

"You can say that again!"

"I'm revolting!"

My plan is really coming together! thought Madame W.

The mattresses flew through the door and slid to a halt in the yard.

"You can't fool me, evil belly-haters!" cried Grub.

"Yeah! You tell 'em, Generalissimo!" cheered Honeybaked.

To the humans, of course, these words sounded more like *Woof, woof, woofing woofers!* and *Squeak, squeak, squeak-ity squeak!*

38

PETLANDIA

CHAPTER FOUR

The humans pounded on the doors and windows, but the pets ignored them. After boarding up the doggy door, Madame Wigglesworth climbed onto Mr. Finkleblurt's favorite chair.

"The reign of terror is over!" she declared. "The palace is ours! From this day forward it shall be known as PETLANDIA!"

"PETLANDIA!" cried the others.

Madame Wigglesworth quickly wrote the Petlandia Declaration of Independence, the Constitution, and the national anthem.

"Hail, hail, Petlandia!
Land that I love,
Land that I'll rule,
Like a queen from above!

"Wait, did I say that? Heh, heh. What I mean, of course, is that we will have free and fair elections, since this is a democracy. Obviously!"

All the pets cheered, "Hail, hail, Petlandia!"

Madame Wigglesworth was getting excited. It was time for step three, the final step.

"First order of business," purred Madame Wigglesworth. "We must elect a president!"

I can't wait to start giving orders and getting pampered, she thought. *Let's see: pedicure, massage, dessert.*

But Madame Wigglesworth forgot one small, teeny-tiny, little, itty-bitty detail: Unlike her, Grub was lovable.

He was immediately elected president by a landslide.

Madame Wigglesworth was horrified.

"The thrill of victory!" screamed Honeybaked.

"The even bigger thrill of Madame Wigglesworth's defeat!" bubbled Clowny.

"Me? President?" gasped Grub. "I can't believes it!"

"I can't believes it way more than you can't believes it," muttered Madame Wigglesworth.

Honeybaked seemed like she might explode with excitement. "I knewed him way backs when he was just a young general in the great Petlandia Revolution of, let's see, ten or fifteen minutes ago! Speech, President Grub! Speech!"

Grub smiled shyly and cleared his throat. "Wows. Me is president. This be proving anybody can grows up to be president! It's a dream come true!"

"It's a nightmare," said Madame Wigglesworth.

"From now on, feller citizens," Grub continued, "we keeps all the good stinks! Not wash them away like the dumb belly-haters with mops! And no more scary vacuum thing! I hereby says that from this day till forever, Petlandia is a clean-free zone!"

"His speechifying is pure poetry!" cheered Honeybaked.

"Gee, thanks," said Grub. "This is the greatest day since I threw up on the mailman."

"Oh, man!" screamed Honeybaked. "That was my favorite-est day till now, too! Here's to Grub being president forever!"

CHAPTER FIVE

"Who wants to eat alls the junk in the 'frigerator and garbage pail, no matter if we is actually hungry or even like the kinda junk it is?" asked President Grub.

"But it's not even dinnertime!" objected Madame Wigglesworth. "It's the middle of the night!"

"I says from now on the kitchen be open twenty-four sevens! And also maybe we throw foods at each other just a little bit, too?" said Grub.

"Yes and yes!" squealed Honeybaked. "Let's vote!"

"I vote absolutely NOT!" shrieked the angry and exasperated feline.

Guess who won.

Two minutes and forty-five seconds later, Grub, Honeybaked, and Clowny emerged from the kitchen, covered with a variety of sauces, gravies, condiments, and multicolored jams and jellies.

"That was so yum!" President Grub hollered. "The frozen pea and salsa milk shake was the best! Even if it did burn my tongue and freeze my brain!"

"Brain? What brain?" grumbled Madame Wigglesworth.

"I gotsa idea!" announced President Grub. "A chandelier-swinging contest in the dining room is the first order of bidness of the Grub adminnerstration! But holds it. We gotsta vote!"

"I vote *definitely!*" shrieked Honeybaked. "Can I vote again?!"

"NO!" screamed Madame Wigglesworth. "ONE VOTE EACH!"

"I vote absolutely!" said Clowny.

"I vote, like, *duh!*" said the most honorable president of Petlandia.

I vote I cannot take this for one more minute, thought Madame Wigglesworth. *But my plan is still perfect. It just needs another step or two. No big deal.*

Think,
Wigglesworth,
think!

CHAPTER SIX

The next morning, Madame Wigglesworth was still thinking, which was difficult due to the horrible racket going on.

"Turning up the music so loud that ever'body's brain sorta rattles around in their head is the bestest law we've passed yet, Mr. President!" screamed Honeybaked.

"She's right, Madame Wigglesworth!" sang Grub.

"Come over and get your grooviness on! I want all Petlandians to participa-tate! How 'bout I nommernate you for my Secretary of Funky Mojo Hippie Hoppin' Hootenannies?!"

"Heh, heh . . ." snickered Madame Wigglesworth. "Hippie Hoppin' Hootenannies . . . all the citizens to participa-tate. Very amusing . . . wait a minute!" She had an idea. "Thank you, Mr. President. I'd be honored to serve, but as it happens, it's time for me to run a little errand! Toodle-oo!"

Actually, it's time to insert a few extra-specially sneaky steps into my plan. Now it simply cannot fail. In fact, I would like to offer my congratulations to me in advance. Why, thank you, me. You're welcome, me.

CHAPTER SEVEN

Madame Wigglesworth descended into the damp, dirty Basemental Territories

It was horribly un-Wigglesworthy. The only light down there was the super-depressing kind with a broken chain attached to a bare bulb, which she couldn't possibly reach.

"Yoo-hoo!" she whispered, peering into the blackness. "Is anyone there?"

The only response was heavy breathing. The super-creepy kind. Madame Wigglesworth trembled all over. Her knees knocked, her whiskers vibrated, and her fur stood on end. Her bones rattled and her flesh tingled with terror.

She was scared. But if she died of fright, so be it. She was on a mission.

"Mr. U, is that you?"

"Not exactly your neck of the woods, is it, Madame Fancypants," said a large gray rat named Ugly, who stepped from the shadows to reveal himself in all his un-glory. "What are you, slumming?"

"No, no, not at all. I quite enjoy your little . . . um . . . subdivision. This neighborhood has simply loads of character. The filth . . . the remarkable variety of stinks and stenches. It's quite charming in its own—how do you say?—horribly nauseating way."

"Quit the chitchat, Fancypantsy. What's on your mind?"

55

"Yes, well, I've always been fond of you and your brothers and I've been thinking about how you should get more involved in the community. I bring news from Upstairsville. The house is no longer a house. Now it's an entire sovereign nation called Petlandia. And as one of its citizens, you are entitled to certain rights."

"Uh-huh," said Mr. Ugly. "Tell that to the humans. They've tried to trap me, poison me, whack me with Wiffle bats, and stomp me with army boots. They're a crazed bunch of homicidal maniacs."

"I know, Uggy!" said Madame Wigglesworth. "The family is evil! They're the *enemy*! But the good news is I'm on your side. And you know what? The humans have been deposed!"

Mr. Ugly stared at her blankly. "What's this 'deposed'? Don't go throwing ten-dollar words around, pussycat. I'm a simple rat with simple needs: food, shelter, and deep, delicious disgustingness. Give it to me straight."

"Certainly," said Madame Wigglesworth. "'Deposed' means kicked out. As in, we kicked the family out on their lazy, greedy rumps. And I guarantee you they are not coming back. Ever. It's a new era, Uggster! The dawn of a brand-new day!"

"Hail, hail, Petlandia!"

Mr. Ugly squinted. "Okay, Fancy-schmancy-pants," he said. "But here's my concern. I notice that the word 'Petlandia' has the word 'pet' right there in it and I am not technically a pet. So how do I fit into this whole Petlandia deal?"

"Aha! That's where I come in," said Madame Wigglesworth. "You see, I'm in tight with the people in charge, because I *am* the people in charge! *I* say who is and isn't a citizen, who gets to stroll freely through our fair nation in broad daylight . . . no longer skulking in shadows like some kind of ugly rat. Wait, strike that. I mean like an *outsider*! Because now you'll be an *insider*!

"You'll be able to waltz into the kitchen, for instance, and make yourself a yummy sandwich out of mountains of leftovers, dripping with chicken fat or marmalade or chocolate syrup, any old time you want! Or maybe polish off a whole can of whipped cream . . . aim that baby directly into your mouth. I happen to know there's a fresh, shiny can of the frothy nectar calling out to you. As. We. Speak."

Mr. Ugly's eyes went weird. He shivered and drifted off to Chicken-Fat-Whipped-Cream Yum-Yum Land. He sweated and panted and drooled. It was gross.

"As . . . we . . . speak?" he asked, feeling a little wobbly.

"Well," said Madame Wigglesworth. "As I speak and you drool. But listen, I've always known that you're a whole lot smarter than anyone gives you credit for.

"You're cultured. You're deep. And you're very, very sensitive.

"You have the soul of a poet . . ."

63

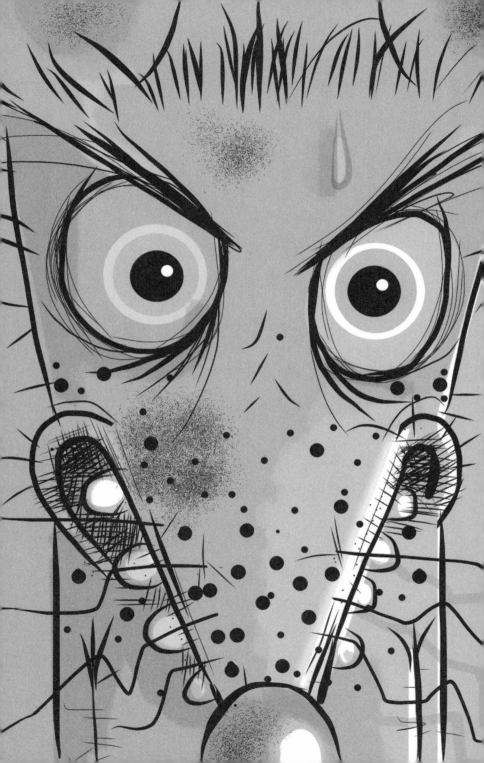

She'd gone too far. Mr. Ugly's eyes suddenly got normal again. "Hold on there. Who are you kidding? I'm none of those things. I'm dirty. I'm disgusting. And I smell bad. My full name is Ugly P. Fartsmello, for heaven's sake. And you are the fanciest cat this side of Fancytown. I repulse you and you know it. You've even said so on many occasions. So, the question is . . .

"WHAT DO YOU WANT FROM ME?!"

"Oh, Uggster," she said. "I thought you'd never ask. All I want is to bestow upon you all the happiness you deserve and I expect absolutely nothing in return. Except for one teeny-tiny favor . . . maybe just a touch of the sneaky, if you don't mind."

"Mind? My middle name might as well be Touch of the Sneaky. I mean, it's not . . . it's Putrid, but you know what I mean."

"Do I ever, Mr. Ugly Putrid Fartsmello. Do I ever."

CHAPTER EIGHT

"Yoo-hoo, I'm back!" called Madame Wigglesworth. "But my paws sure ache from that long trip to the distant Basemental Territories. Maybe President Grub would like to massage my tootsies a bit?"

"Gee, thanks for the offer," said Grub, "but we gotsta stuff socks and undies down the toilet and flush like a zillion times to flood the bathroom and hallway. Then we're gonna run the rapids in pots and pans while shooting off firecrackers and screaming at the top of our lungs."

"Good plan, Mr. President," said Madame Wigglesworth. "I suppose we should probably vote? Let's see . . . I guess I'll vote no. I cannot fathom how you other fine citizens will come down on this issue."

"We vote YES!" cried Grub, Honeybaked, and Clowny.

"The yesses win!" squealed Honeybaked. "Our yesses will always beat her nos!"

"What's her nose gotsta do with it?" asked the president.

"Hold on," said Madame Wigglesworth. "Not everyone has voted yet."

"But alls of us is here, silly-billy," said Grub.

"Not everyone," said Madame Wigglesworth, throwing open the basement door to reveal three huge rats.

"Wow," said Honeybaked. "They sure is ugly, scary, and disgusting."

"Yes, as a matter of fact," said Madame Wigglesworth, "I'd like you to meet my associates, Ugly, Scary, and Disgusting Fartsmello.

"These strapping young brothers hail from a lovely little subdivision in the enchanting nether regions of Petlandia. All right, Brothers Fartsmello! Time to cast your votes!"

"Uh . . . what was that again?" asked Disgusting.

Madame Wigglesworth rolled her eyes and whispered something to the three brothers.

"Oh, right," said Ugly. "We all vote *no* on the river thing and a big enthusiastic *yes* on the paw-rubbing thing. Do we get paid now?"

"Shhhhhh," hissed Madame Wigglesworth.

CHAPTER NINE

"This is not nearlys as fun as pretty much everything else in Petlandia," said Grub.

"Yeah," said Honeybaked. "I don't really think the president of a whole entire country should have to do this kind of thing."

"You know," said Madame Wigglesworth, "I agree."

"You does?" asked Honeybaked.

"Yes," she replied. "I think it's time for a new election. The old one is no longer valid since our delightful young Fartsmellos here have developed an interest in politics. Okay. Who wants Grub and who wants me? You know what? There's really no need to vote. Fartsmellos are straight feline voters from way back. It's four to three. Meet President Wigglesworth."

Something is fishy in Petlandia and I'm not just talking about me.

TEAM GRUB

"Wait," said Grub sadly. "If I not president no more, then what is I?"

"Why, you're the best paw massager in all of Petlandia!" said President Wigglesworth.

So Grub did a whole lot more paw massaging. And claw polishing. And litter scooping. He even did some *belly* rubbing—something he truly missed and didn't know President Wigglesworth even *liked*.

Honeybaked served the president breakfast, lunch, dinner, and snacks. Lots and lots of snacks. Clowny washed dishes. As soon as he finished one sinkful, another was ready to go. "This is exactly like my normal horrible life, except now I'm also eating soap all day."

It was nonstop misery all around.

Except for President Wigglesworth. She was living the life to which she had always dreamed she'd become accustomed.

CHAPTER TEN

But as everyone knows, foot-rubbing leads to relaxation, which leads to drowsiness and sleep. And eventually, President Wigglesworth went out like a big, fat, furry light.

Honeybaked snuck away. She trekked to Attica, high in the upper reaches of the Petlandia Highlands.

"The air being so thin up here, I is a little dizzy," she said. "I even forgetted why I came. Wait. I know!

"HEY, YOUSE BATS!"

she said in her loudest, happiest, looniest voice.

"CAN WE TALK?!"

Honeybaked heard the rustling of wings.

"*You* can talk, as long as you do it somewhere else, far, far away!" shrieked Randall, the father of a lovely family of British bats, rubbing his beady red eyes. "We're trying to sleep, you wingless twit!"

"SLEEP! You gotsta be kiddin' me! It's nearly the crack o' noon! Does all you English types snooze the whole day away?"

"English-type bats do!" shrieked Madge, the mother. "*All* bats are nocturnal. Which means your day is our night and your night is our day!"

This woke Billy, the baby of the family. He looked down at the agitated hamster. "Exactly what sort of nitwit *are* you?!" he screeched in a voice so high the attic window exploded.

"I is exactly no sort of nitwit. I is a high-functioning nincompoop!"

"And I just come to tell you this house is a whole new nation called Petlandia. Grub was president (and I L-word him, but that's a secret) and now Lady McWigglesworth stealed it from him, but you don't care because alls you cares about is your stupid beauty sleep, which, by the ways, *isn't working!* Good-bye!"

"WAIT!" screeched Madge, dropping to the floor with a thud. "Did you say Wigglesworth? I hate that hideous feline with a passion. She refers to Billy as the Rabies Baby! I wish *I* had rabies. I'd bite her in the you-know-what!"

"I actually don't know what," said Billy.

"Never you mind," said Madge. "The main thing is we are with Team Grub all the way!"

"Yay, Grub!" screeched the whole bat family.

"Thank goodness," said Honeybaked. "That is music to my ears. High-pitched screechy music that breaks windows and makes my brain hurt and teeth ache slightly, but still music . . ."

Madge winced. "Okay, okay. Grub has our support if you will please stop talking. Right now!"

Five minutes later, Grub regained the presidency.

CHAPTER ELEVEN

But it was short-lived. Squirrels are easy to convince when it comes to voting against dogs.

"But President Grub love the squirrelies," he sighed. "He just like the chasing, not the catching!"

"You said once that you wanted to put mustard and relish on my tail and chew it off!" said one of them.

"I meant that in the niceyest possible way!" said Grub.

"You're out on your ear, Paw Massager, Claw Polisher, Litter Scooper, and Belly Rubber!" said Madame Wigglesworth. "The furry little rodent-people have spoken."

But Grub went campaigning for more support, too. And he didn't have to go far. He found a large neighborhood of frogs in the garage.

"Fresh flies in every pot!" he promised. "And by the way, I happy to kiss your babies and change them into princes and princesses, if that is the kinda empty-ish promise you is looking for!"

President Grub was back in power.

CHAPTER TWELVE

Madame Wigglesworth thought she was as miserable as she could get, but just then, President Grub and Honeybaked Hamster conga'd by with twenty-nine demented frogs, all hopped up on the promise that their children would feast on fresh-fly sandwiches served on a silver platter by a deeply disgruntled cat.

Hail to the chief!

Madame Wigglesworth blew a gasket. A very important one. The one that keeps the wackadoodle from seeping into one's brain.

Petlandia has slipped into chaos! she screamed to herself. *Seriously stupid chaos. But this stupidity will not stand! And it certainly will not continue to conga!*

Love to the chief!

Oh, the stupidity!

"The entire democratic process has broken down!" she screamed. "What happened to the will of the people? And by that I mean the will of *me*! *What the hair balls is going on?* Petlandia has gone one-hundred-percent bonkers! I mean, *Grub*? Leader of a *nation*? Please! And no thank you!

"I need more votes and I need them now!"

94

CHAPTER THIRTEEN

Madame Wigglesworth peered through a crack in the boarded-up doggy door. A light rain was falling. The family was nowhere to be seen. They must have finally given up and left. "Well, at least *something* is going as planned," she hissed.

She pried off as many boards as she could—breaking several claws in the process—and ended up with a too-small hole, through which she attempted to squeeze her body like toothpaste from a tube.

She got stuck halfway. She wriggled and flapped her arms like a loony bird. She made loud, rhythmic grunting noises through her teeth, nose, ears, and possibly pores. Then finally Madame Wigglesworth popped through the hole like a cork from a bottle.

She made a one-point landing.

Head pounding and nose bloodied, Madame Wigglesworth crawled through the mud on her belly like a reptile . . . something a model of elegance such as herself would never dream of doing under normal circumstances. But this was an epic battle for control of Petlandia, a cause worth getting down and dirty for.

In fact, she was about to do something *way down* and *way dirtier!*

She started digging up the lawn . . .
like . . . like a . . . *dog*! A lowly mutt
wallowing in the mud!

It was so beneath her, so unbelievably yucky! But desperate times call for desperately yucky measures!

"It's for the greater good!" she cried through clenched teeth. "I mean *my* greater good!" she corrected, digging deeper still.

Then she disappeared into the earth.

Four long minutes later, she resurfaced like a swimmer gasping for air. A very filthy swimmer with forty-two wriggling earthworms clenched delicately between her teeth. This was by far the low point of Madame Wigglesworth's political life. Also life life.

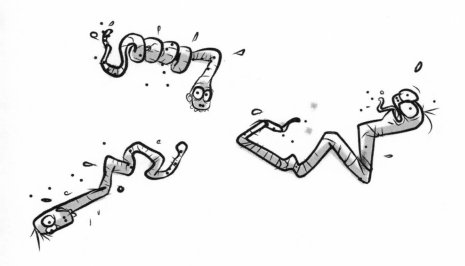

"That mutt will pay for this," she seethed. "And you," she said to her wiggly mouthful of new voters, "do not even think of betraying me. I've already come this far. Chewing you up and spitting you out would be no big whoop. I know where the humans keep the toothpaste. And the floss!"

I can't believe I just said that, she thought. *Worse yet, I meant it!*

She paused and shut her eyes tightly, hoping to somehow erase the image of freshly chewed worms stuck between her perfect teeth. She was woozy with nausea. She thought she might lose it. But she couldn't lose it. She was no loser!

"Excuse me, fearless leader, my name is Harold," said a young worm, rising from the cat's lips like an animated noodle. "I don't think I'm even old enough to vote. I'm only thirteen. Weeks, that is."

Madame Wigglesworth had no time for this.

"Listen, Harold, is it? Worm weeks are different from regular weeks. So, lucky you. Not only are you old enough to vote, you're halfway to the grave."

Harold was horrified. "You call that *lucky?*"

"I sure do!" said Madame Wigglesworth. "I rescued you from the muck! Most worms would give their right arms for that. I mean, their right sides where they'd have arms if they weren't worms! Come on! I'm transporting you free of charge to the booming republic of Petlandia! If you aren't tired, poor, huddled masses yearning to breathe free, who is?! Show a little gratitude! You are partaking in the wonders of democracy!"

"I don't know," said Harold with a grimace. "It feels more like I'm partaking in pain and suffering. Are the wonders of democracy always so sharp and pointy?"

"Wake up and smell the dirt, Harold! You're a worm! Anything that doesn't involve getting squished by a tire or stabbed by a fish hook is a luxury vacation for you!"

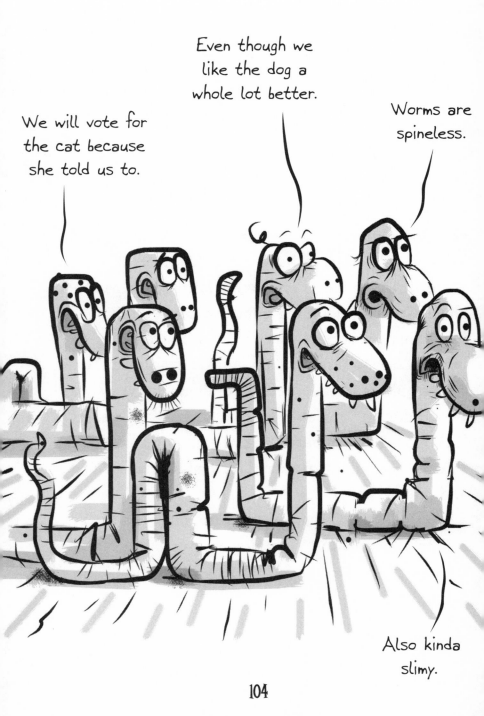

CHAPTER FOURTEEN

So Madame Wigglesworth got the worm vote. Except for Harold, but it didn't matter.

It wasn't even close.

"Guess who's president once again?" she laughed, causing a mud clod to fire from her nostril like a wet bullet.

"Wait just one second, Wigglesworth," said Honeybaked. "How'd you get so dirty-ish all of a sudden?"

"I have no idea what you're talking about," said Wigglesworth, shaking mud from her mangy fur.

"Yard mud!" squealed Honeybaked. "These worms are *Yard* Dwellers, not *House* Dwellers, so they cannot vote!"

"Wrong, rodent! Check your Constitution! It's all in there in black and white with red cross-outs and scribbled additions!"

"I see!" cried Honeybaked. "So you *changed* the Constitution!"

"Make that *'amended'*! Because, unlike some people whose names start with 'GR' and end with 'UB,' I know a thing or two about leadership. This dog is a nitwit!"

Honeybaked was livid. "Oh, yeah?! Well, 'nitwit' ends with 'wit' and 'wit' means 'smart'! So there!"

"Yeah, well, a *nit* is the egg of a *louse*, so Grub is as smart as a *louse*. And twice as *lousy!*"

"Excuse me," said Grub, getting very confused, "I not really following this conbersation so good. What does nits and wits and lousy eggs has to do with Petlandia?"

107

"Ha! You see!" howled Madame Wigglesworth. "He can't follow a simple conversation! Do we really want a leader who is so unaware, so uninformed, so utterly unpresidential? He's a bonehead, a blockhead, a dunderhead! He's slow as a snail! Make that a glacier! He's as sharp as a marshmallow, and I'm talking about a *melted* marshmallow . . ."

This went on for some time. She was very prolific when it came to insults.

Honeybaked Hamster was not amused.

It was as if these terrible things were being said about *her.*

Actually, it was worse.

CHAPTER FIFTEEN

"Why, you gigantic pile of WRONG!" she cried, leaping like a tiny ninja. She made a lot of phony martial arts yells and motions, but the main thing was she chomped her razor-sharp teeth into the president of Petlandia's nose with all her might.

This turn of events was such a shock, at first Madame Wigglesworth didn't even react.

Then she let out an unearthly howl. She shook her head violently, but Honeybaked hung on for dear life, her teeth sinking ever deeper into tender feline schnoz flesh.

"My nose! My beautiful nose!" cried President Wigglesworth. "Listen, rodent! This is not the behavior one should display at a presidential face-to-face! Not to mention:

"OWW! OUCHY! ALSO: OUCH!"

"GRRRRRR!" said Honeybaked. It's hard to talk with a mouthful of nose.

"THAT'S TREASON!" screamed the president.

"THAT'S ENTERTAINMENT!" shouted Ugly or Scary or Disgusting. Definitely a Fartsmello, anyway. "We don't get a lotta channels down in the Basemental Territories!"

The worms and frogs and rats hooted and hollered, cheering on the battlers. Then they all joined in the mayhem. It was brother against brother, worm against worm, rat against cat against bat against frog. Everybody against everybody. It was a free-for-all.

"CIVIL WAR!" cried the president.

"More like UNCIVIL!" bubbled Clowny.

CHAPTER SIXTEEN

Meanwhile, Grub was completely unaware of all the commotion. He was a dog in a fog, teetering back and forth, babbling gibberish to himself. Then he cocked his head, like he was listening to a voice deep inside. "Really?" he asked some invisible someone. "Uh-huh, uh-huh. Yeah, okay, yuh-huh . . ."

Honeybaked Hamster and President Wigglesworth stopped fighting. So did all the bats and rats and frogs and worms.

"I think he may have finally lost his beautiful mind," said Honeybaked in a voice laden with deep sadness.

"How can one lose what one never had?" asked the president.

But Madame Wigglesworth had lost a lot herself. Her elegance and dignity were long gone. She was covered with mud and blood. Her fur was matted, her tail mangled, and her once-perfect nose, now permanently perforated by hamster teeth, had swollen to twice its size. Half of her right ear had been gnawed off by frogs, who don't even really have teeth.

Plus she had very bad worm breath.

CHAPTER SEVENTEEN

But Madame Wigglesworth was smiling. She knew it had all been worth it.

"This zombie is clearly no longer a threat to my throne, I mean presidency. I will serve my four-year term and four more after that. By then I will have changed the stupid term-limit laws. Why deprive my subjects of a great queen, I mean, *leader*? I'll reign, I mean *serve,* for at least nine lives. Petlandia is mine, all mine."

Honeybaked Hamster wept. The object of her admiration and affection had drifted off to loony land. It was a sad, sad sight. A great light had gone out, plunging Petlandia into darkness.

Honeybaked threw her head back and shook her tiny fists at the heavens. "SOMEBODY! GIVE ME ONE GOOD-ISH REASON WHY LIFE ISN'T A BIG BOWL OF ROTTEN CHERRIES! A BIG STINKEROO!"

Her words echoed off the walls, ceilings, and floors of Petlandia.

But no answer came.

CHAPTER EIGHTEEN

Until Grub spoke. "I gotsa reason. And a idea."

Honeybaked closed her eyes and sighed. "Now, now, you poor, deluded dear. You only *thinking* you gotsa idea. You brainy not really in the thinking or idea business no more."

But Grub was wide-awake now. "No, I pretty sure I gots one. Turns out some a my friends are intere-tested in the political processor, and every single one, all 2,437 of them, want to vote. For me. My fleas, I mean."

"GRUB! YOU'RE BACK!" squeaked Honeybaked, leaping off Wigglesworth's head, bouncing off her throbbing nose ("Ouch again!") and onto the floor. She looked up at her hero. "I stand before you, profounded-ly humbled by your genius-ness! And wait! Hold on!" She knocked on her head like it was a door. "Hello? Yes? Great news! My three fleas are on board, too!"

With that, 2,440 fleas screamed at the top of their lungs.

You needed to lean in close to hear, but the results were undeniable. Commander-in-Chief Grub was back on the job.

122

"Okie-doke," he said. "On with the bidness of gubberment! We needs bigger ideas!"

"Ooh! Ooh!" said Honeybaked, getting all worked up again. "I gots one! I place into nommernation 'Chase the Cat' as the official national sport of Petlandia!"

"YES!" howled the president.

"WAIT!" screamed Clowny.

"FINALLY!" cried Wigglesworth. "A wise voice crying out in the wilderness!"

"Right," bubbled Clowny. "If you call one square foot of pink gravel and a hunk of plastic seaweed 'wilderness.' Anyway, I move that we guarantee that all Petlandian clown fishes—that's me—shall be carried to and fro, so as to fully partake in any and all matches of the sport known as Chase the Cat!"

"ALL IN FLAVOR?!" said Grub.

"YES, YES, A THOUSAND TIMES YES!" screamed a clear majority of the registered lunatics.

Then they noticed that Madame Wigglesworth was grinning again. Always a bad sign.

"You didn't really think you had Wigglesworth beat, did you?" she cackled. "Congrats on your little flea stunt, but say hello to my little friends: 35 million flying, creeping, crawling insects. It's hard to keep track. They keep multiplying."

"The final election results are in," she continued. "And now that my flying creepy-crawlers have cast their ballots, it's all over. Their babies' babies' babies will be having babies just about . . . four, three, two, one . . . *now*. We're registering a thousand new voters a second."

One minute later, President For-Ever-and-Always Madame Wigglesworth was relaxing in a warm bubble bath, balancing a bowl of gourmet vanilla ice cream on her paw. "People, did I not request hot fudge, crushed nuts, and a minimum of one measly maraschino cherry? Think, people, think! And Official Doer-of-Whatever-I-Told-You-to-Do-Most-Recently, why have you stopped working? You've barely even started your rest-of-your-life shift!"

"Me hears a
curious something.
Anybody else hears a
curious something?"

"Oh, for sure,"
said Honeybaked. "I
definitely hears a very
curious something."

Then everyone heard a loud splintering . . .
something.

President Wigglesworth poked her head out of
the bubbles and summoned her brain trust.

"Brothers Fartsmello! I need a breakdown of Petlandia's population! Pronto!"

Disgusting squinted at a computer printout. He was the one Fartsmello who actually was a smart fellow. "We are .02 percent mammal, 1.4 percent reptile, 4.7 percent amphibian, and the rest insect . . . just about 94 percent. And 99 percent of *those* are termites. Plus or minus .3 termites."

"What precisely is a point-three termite?" asked the president.

"Precisely disgusting," said Disgusting. "Anyway, of that 99 percent, 100 percent are hungry. And I'm pretty sure they're all having lunch right now."

This was followed by unbelievably loud crashing, screaming, and ouching sounds.

CHAPTER NINETEEN

After the dust had cleared, nobody was president because Petlandia was no more.

Madame Wigglesworth couldn't believe it. Her brilliant plan had worked, but in the end it hadn't mattered. "I've heard that all great nations eventually fall," she said. "But right onto our heads?"

130

"Yeah, plus raindrops are falling on our heads also," said Grub.

A mysterious finger summoned them to the doghouse.

The rain was coming down hard now, but Madame Wigglesworth would not budge.

"I will not even consider sharing that pathetic structure with a lunatic and a family of evil humans."

"I is totally fine with it," said Grub, "since I *is* the lunatic and I guess I *likes* evil humans!"

"Me too!" squeaked Honeybaked Hamster.

"Whatever," bubbled Clowny. "I'm wet and depressed wherever I am!"

It was a lovefest.

All four Finkleblurts rubbed Grub's belly. He closed his eyes to bask in the adoration.

"I knowed they still loves me."

Honeybaked hesitated, but then worked up her courage: "Um, President Grub, I thinks it's time I tolds you that I loves you, too."

"Yup, I knows," said Grub.

The love-struck hamster shook like a leaf and gushed tears of joy. "You knew all along?"

"A course," he said. "*Everyone* loves me." But Madame Wigglesworth didn't believe in all that love junk. "Getting all mushy about a bunch of yokels you supposedly give a hoot about is for chumps."

"Okay, but is you comin' in?" asked Grub.

"Not in a million years!"

"Okay, then hows about right now?"

"Hello? Do you even *own* a pair of ears? Or did they somehow get disconnected from your head during the Great Battle of Petlandia?"

"Nope, still gots 'em. They just don't work so good when a ocean of water is crashing down from the sky."

"Okay! I'll speak loudly and slowly then! I WILL NEVER . . . EVER . . . *EVER* . . . SET FOOT IN THERE!"

"I sorry," said Grub. "I dozed off for a second. Was you sayin' something?"

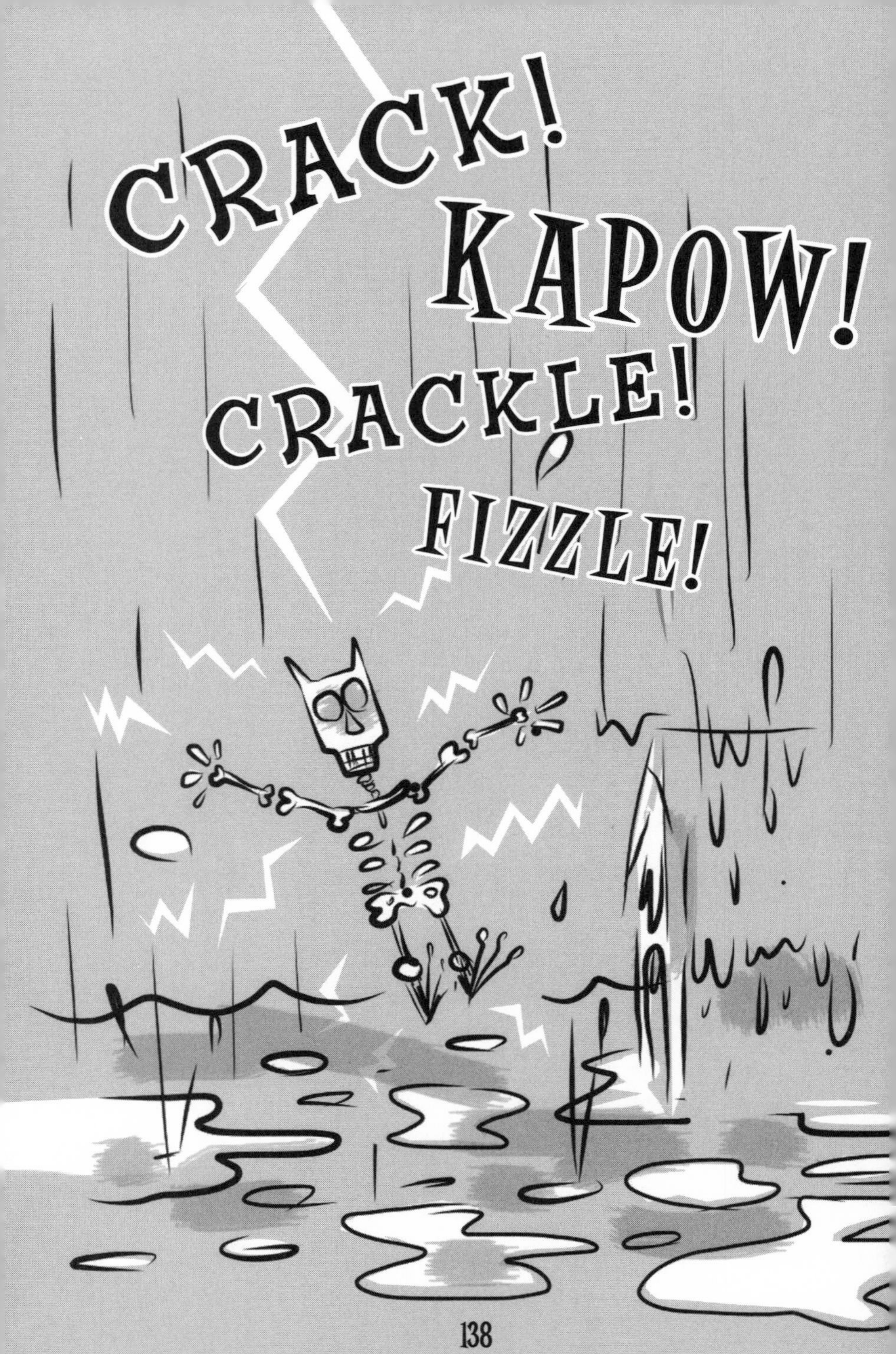
CRACK!
KAPOW!
CRACKLE!
FIZZLE!

"Okay, maybe I went a tad overboard with that whole 'never' thing."

"Welcome to our cozy-ish little home sweet home!" said Grub.

"Is that your idea of a joke?" asked Madame Wigglesworth. "It's stinky and soggy, we're packed in like sardines with the evil humans, and I feel another attack of stark-raving nutjob-itis coming on."

THE END

PETER HANNAN

created the Nickelodeon animated series *CatDog*. He also wrote and sang the show's theme song. He is the author/illustrator of *My Big Mouth: 10 Songs I Wrote That Almost Got Me Killed*; the Super Goofballs series; *Freddy, King of Flurb*; *The Greatest Snowman in the World; Escape From Camp Wannabarf*; and *The Adventures of a Huge Mouth*. His work has appeared in magazines, newspapers, and galleries, and been turned into everything from T-shirts to cheese crackers. He loves pets. He firmly believes that pets should rule the world.

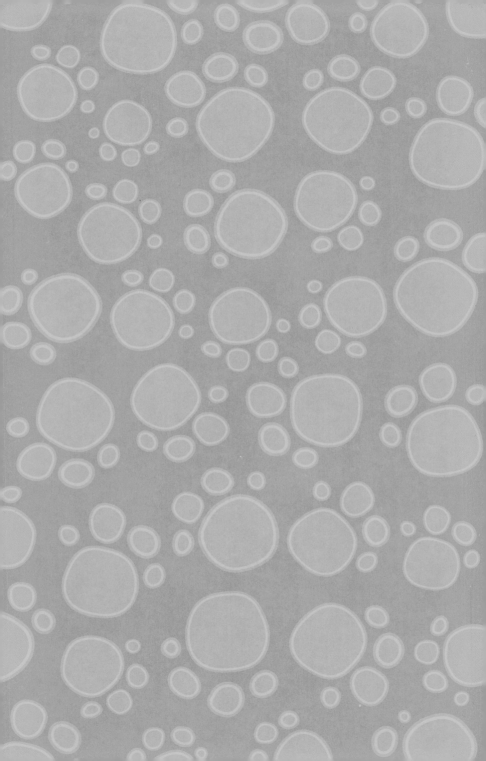